Bloom

Bloom

Written by
Kevin Panetta

Artwork by
Savanna Ganucheau

:01

First Second
New York

First Second

Text copyright © 2019 by Kevin Panetta
Illustrations copyright © 2019 by Savanna Ganucheau

Published by First Second
First Second is an imprint of Roaring Brook Press, a division of Holtzbrinck
Publishing Holdings Limited Partnership
175 Fifth Avenue, New York, NY 10010

Don't miss your next favorite book from First Second!
Sign up for our enewsletter to get updates at firstsecondnewsletter.com.

Library of Congress Control Number: 2018937127

Paperback ISBN: 978-1-62672-641-3
Hardcover ISBN: 978-1-250-19691-0

Our books may be purchased in bulk for promotional, educational, or business use.
Please contact your local bookseller or the Macmillan Corporate and Premium Sales Department
at (800) 221-7945 ext. 5442 or by email at MacmillanSpecialMarkets@macmillan.com.

First edition, 2019

Edited by Calista Brill and Sarah Gaydos
Book design by Molly Johanson

Bloom was completely rendered in Photoshop. Inked using GrutBrushes's "papaya grind"
and toned with Kyle T. Webster's halftone brushes.

Printed in the United States of America by Worzalla, Stevens Point, Wisconsin

Paperback: 10 9 8 7 6 5 4 3 2
Hardcover: 10 9 8 7 6 5 4 3 2 1

YOU DOING OKAY THERE, LITTLE BRO?

HUH? OH, YEAH. I'M FINE. I JUST DANCED MYSELF TO SLEEP.

I STILL CAN'T BELIEVE YOU'RE **MARRIED.**

I KNOW. IT'S CRAZY, RIGHT?

HEY. COME WITH ME FOR A SECOND. I WANNA TALK TO YOU.

JEEZ! WHY IS MY FAMILY MANHANDLING ME AT THIS WEDDING?

AND WHY ARE WE GOING SOMEWHERE?

BECAUSE I'M THE BRIDE **AND** YOUR BIG SISTER, SO YOU HAVE TO DO WHAT I SAY.

JUST SIT DOWN FOR A MINUTE.

I'LL BE RIGHT BACK.

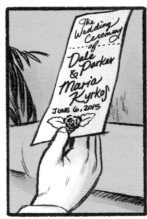

The Wedding Ceremony of Dale Parker & Maria Kyrkos
JUNE 6, 2015

HOW'S DALE HANDLING TODAY? HE'S...OKAY?

HUH?

HE'S FINE, I GUESS?

WHAT? NONONONO. I JUST KNOW YOU GUYS HAVE BEEN UP AND DOWN RECENTLY. I WAS JUST ASKING, THAT'S ALL.

MHM.

THAT'S JUST HOW RELATIONSHIPS GO, ARI. THEY AREN'T ALWAYS EASY. YOU HAVE TO PUT WORK INTO THEM.

ANYWAY, I DIDN'T BRING YOU UP HERE TO TALK ABOUT DALE.

IT'S ABOUT YOU.

MOM SAID YOU'RE PLANNING ON MOVING AWAY.

DO YOU REALLY THINK THAT'S THE BEST THING RIGHT NOW?

OH, GOD.

YOU SOUND LIKE DAD.

DAD ISN'T **ALWAYS** WRONG, YOU KNOW.

HE'S TOLD YOU TO BREAK UP WITH DALE LIKE FIVE DIFFERENT TIMES AND NOW YOU'RE MARRIED.

SO HE'S DEFINITELY **SOMETIMES** WRONG.

HAH

OKAY, SMARTASS.

LOOK, I'M JUST SAYING. I'M MOVING OUT. THE BAKERY ISN'T DOING GREAT. MOM AND DAD ARE GONNA NEED SOME HELP.

tep
tep
tep
tep

HOW LONG DO YOU GUYS THINK I COULD WALK LIKE THIS?

FIVE HOURS!

THIS IS BORING.

CHALLENGE... ACCEPTED.

LAUREN, HOW ARE YOU BORED?

WE JUST PARTIED AND DANCED WITH A BUNCH OF COOL PEOPLE.

YEAH. BUT PEOPLE ARE THE WORST.

ESPECIALLY IN THIS TOWN.

BUT YOU'RE NOT EVEN THE SINGER.

ARE YOU SERIOUS?!

COME ON. SIT WITH ME AND LET ME TALK TO YOU FOR A SECOND.

WITH YOUR SISTER GONE, I'M GOING TO NEED YOU TO STEP IT UP AROUND HERE.

BUT I'M LEAVING. CAMERON IS ALREADY LOOKING FOR PLACES AND—

THIS ISN'T A GOOD TIME FOR THAT, ARI.

BE SENSIBLE.

JUST BECAUSE YOU WANT SOMETHING DOESN'T MEAN I WANT THE SAME THING.

I KNOW THE BAKERY IS YOUR WHOLE LIFE, BUT I WANT TO DO THIS BAND.

I WANTED TO GO TO SCHOOL FOR MUSIC, BUT WE COULDN'T AFFORD IT.

SO THIS IS WHAT I'M DOING INSTEAD.

I'M MOVING WITH CAMERON AND EVERYBODY TO THE CITY TO TRY TO MAKE THIS HAPPEN.

I KNOW YOU WANTED TO GO TO SCHOOL, SON.

WE TRIED TO MAKE IT WORK, I PROMISE YOU THAT.

I WISH WE HAD ALL THE MONEY IN THE WORLD, BUT THE TRUTH IS, WE BARELY HAVE ENOUGH TO KEEP GOING RIGHT NOW.

I KNOW. I KNOW.

I DIDN'T MEAN ANYTHING BAD.

I JUST REALLY WANT TO TRY TO MAKE THIS BAND HAPPEN.

GAMOTO.

UNF

LOOK...WHAT IF I FIND SOMEONE TO REPLACE ME?

SOMEONE REALLY GOOD TO HELP YOU GUYS OUT AFTER I LEAVE?

YOU DON'T LISTEN. WE NEED YOU **HERE**.

WE ARE NOT TALKING ABOUT THIS RIGHT NOW, ARI.

IT'S TIME FOR YOU TO GET TO WORK.

BUT...

FINE.

SLAM

SOURDOU
START

click

WRRRRR

KOFF

KOFF

WHRRRRRR

VRRRRR

CALLING
THE EGG

AHHH!! HECTOR!!

HOW ARE YOU!?

HOW'S THE BEACH?!

TELL ME EVERYTHING!

OH MY GOD, MEG.

YOU HAVE SO MUCH **ENERGY** RIGHT NOW.

HAHA

I'M FINE, THOUGH. I GOT HERE YESTERDAY.

NANA'S HOUSE IS SO FULL OF STUFF. I DON'T EVEN KNOW WHERE TO START.

I'M SO STRESSED OUT.

THAT'S AMAZING!

YOU SHOULD MAKE SOMETHING OUT OF THERE. IT'LL RELAX YOU.

THAT'S ACTUALLY A REALLY GOOD IDEA.

YEAH, WELL... I'M ACTUALLY FULL OF REALLY GOOD IDEAS.

DANGIT!

OKAY, SWEETIE. I'M GONNA GO FIGURE OUT THIS MESS.

YOU STILL GOOD WITH ME **AND** ANDREW COMING OUT TO VISIT?

YEAH! WHY WOULDN'T I BE?

I DON'T KNOW!

HE **DID** GET KIND OF WEIRD ON YOU AT THE END.

LIKE...CLINGY OR SOMETHING.

ISN'T THAT WHAT ALWAYS HAPPENS TO ME?

YEAH, I WONDER WHY THAT HAPPENS... HMMM?

HEY! WHAT'S THAT MEA—

ANYWAY, I'M JUST CHECKING! YOU NEVER KNOW.

OKAY. GOTTA RUN. LOVEYOUBYE.

OH MY GOD **BYEEE!**

FOLD

OKAY! THANK YOU, MR. STERLING!

I'LL TELL MY DAD YOU SAID HI!

DING DING

BEACH COPIES

BANNERS + FLAGS

SIGNS SIGNS SIGN

QUICK COPIES

FLASHING SIGN SOLD HERE

JAKE THE SNAKE!!

CAN YOU NOT CALL ME THAT?

IT SOUNDS LIKE I'M SNEAKY OR EVIL OR SOMETHING.

I DON'T KNOW, MAN. JAKE THE SNAKE WAS PRETTY COOL.

HE HAD A SNAKE!

THAT SOUNDS ALL RIGHT. MAYBE I SHOULD GET A SNAKE.

AND HE HAD A MUSTACHE!

NOPE. DEFINITELY STOP CALLING ME THAT.

FIIINE!

CAN YOU HELP ME, THOUGH?

I WANNA MAKE FLYERS TO HIRE A REPLACEMENT AT THE BAKERY.

DOES THAT MEAN YOU CAN MOVE, DUDE?!

AHHHH!!

DUDE!

I'M SO EXCITED, MAN!

WELL, I HAVE TO HIRE SOMEBODY FIRST, SO IT'S NOT ONE HUNDRED PERCENT OR ANYTHING.

WELL, MI COPY MACHINES ES SU COPY MACHINES, AMIGO!

LET'S GET THIS HIRING SHOW ON THE ROAD!

ACTUALLY...I DON'T HAVE A FLYER YET. I WAS HOPING YOU COULD USE YOUR PHOTOSHOP SKILLS AND HOOK ME UP...?

KINDA...?

OF COURSE YOU WERE.

LOOKS LIKE WE'VE GOT A GOOD CHUNK OF PEOPLE OUT THERE, HON!

THEY LOOK LIKE SOME FUN CHARACTERS!

LOOK AT THESE PEOPLE. LORD SAVE ME.

ARI!

WHAT DID YOU DO?

WHY DO YOU WANT TO WORK IN A BAKERY?

FREE DONUTS, DUDE.

AND DO YOU HAVE ANY EXPERIENCE WORKING IN THE FOOD INDUSTRY?

NO, BUT, LIKE, MY MOM COOKS EVERY DAY, SO I'VE SEEN IT, YOU KNOW? LIKE, I'VE BEEN AROUND IT.

HOW DID YOU FIND OUT ABOUT THE POSITION?

GOD TOLD ME ABOUT IT.

I CAN CONTROL SOUND WITH MY MIND.

WOULD THAT BE HELPFUL?

THANK YOU FOR YOUR TIME.

SO YOU'LL JUST CALL ME AND TELL ME WHEN I START, FELLA?

WE'LL BE IN TOUCH.

Sorry WE'RE Closed

flip

PA HA HA HA HA HA!

IT'S NOT **FUNNY!!**

HA HA HA HA

OH MY GOODNESS.

IT'S **KIND OF** FUNNY.

WHERE DID YOU POST THE FLYERS, BOY? OUTSIDE A LOONY BIN??

IT'S **NOT** FUNNY!

THIS IS IMPORTANT TO ME!

STOMP

STOMP

AND YOU'RE **NOT** SUPPOSED TO CALL IT A **LOONY BIN**! WHAT ARE YOU, **ONE HUNDRED**?!

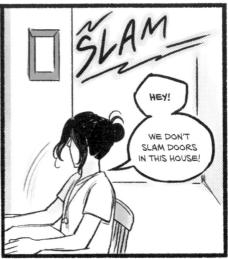

SLAM

HEY!

WE DON'T SLAM DOORS IN THIS HOUSE!

knock knock

ARI. WHAT'S GOING ON?

I THOUGHT IF I FOUND A REPLACEMENT, DAD WOULD LET ME LEAVE.

BUT NOW HE'S JUST MAKING FUN OF ME.

HE THINKS IT'S A JOKE.

WHO? YOUR FATHER?

YOU MIGHT NOT BELIEVE IT, BUT YOUR FATHER WASN'T SO DIFFERENT FROM YOU WHEN HE WAS YOUR AGE.

YOU TRIED TO FIND A SOLUTION TODAY, ARI.

IT DIDN'T WORK OUT, BUT I'M PROUD OF YOU FOR TRYING.

MA, IT'S JUST—

ARI! COME TALK TO ME, NOW!

NO!

STOP ACTING LIKE A BABY!

YOU WANT TO BE A GROWN PERSON?

ACT LIKE ONE AND TALK TO ME!

IT'S FINE. THIS IS FINE.

CAMERON AND HANNA AND EVERYBODY ARE GOING TO THE CITY THIS WEEKEND, ANYWAY, SO I'M JUST GONNA GO WITH THEM.

WHAT?

RIGHT **NOW?**

YEAH.

I GOTTA GET OUT OF HERE.

IT'S JUST FOR A COUPLE OF DAYS. I'LL BE BACK MONDAY.

LOVE YOU, MOM.

I'LL TEXT YOU WHEN I GET THERE.

SUCH A DRAMATIC EXIT.

WELL, HE IS STILL A TEENAGER FOR A LITTLE WHILE LONGER.

IT'S TRUE, BUT SOMETIMES YOU HAVE TO WORK FOR THINGS YOU WANT...

"...WHAT DOES HE THINK IS GOING TO HAPPEN?"

"AN ANGEL WILL JUST FALL FROM THE SKY?"

HECTOR GALEAI! IS THAT YOU?

WELL, LOOK AT YOU! I HAVEN'T SEEN YOU SINCE YOU WERE A LITTLE GUY.

BUT LOOK AT YOU NOW, ALL GROWN UP.

YOU LOOK JUST LIKE YOUR DADDY.

HE WAS QUITE THE HEARTBREAKER WHEN HE WAS YOUR AGE.

I'M SORRY, BUT—

OH! AIN'T I STUPID. OF COURSE YOU WOULDN'T REMEMBER ME!

I'M DEB. DEB LIPINSKI. I USED TO BE GOOD FRIENDS WITH YOUR MOM AND DAD. HAVEN'T TALKED TO EITHER OF THEM IN FOREVER, THOUGH.

HOW THEY DOIN'?

THEY'RE OKAY.

JUST SORT OF DOING THEIR THING.

I HEARD ABOUT YOUR GRANDMA, HON.

IF YOU NEED ANYTHING WHILE YOU'RE IN TOWN, JUST LET ME KNOW.

OKAY!

IT WAS NICE MEETING YOU, BUT I GOTTA RUN!

BYE!

ROAD TRIP!!

HANNA. YOU DON'T HAVE TO YELL "ROAD TRIP" EVERY FIVE MINUTES.

WHAT? WHY?

WE **ARE** ON A ROAD TRIP. I'M JUST TELLING IT LIKE IT IS.

I AM A SPEAKER OF TRUTHS.

SHE HAS A POINT, LAUREN.

OH MY GOD. BOTH OF YOU SHUT UP.

HAHA

HA HA HA

HEY. I MADE A MIX CD FOR THE TRIP.

A CD?!

THAT'S SO CUTE. LEMME SEE.

SPOON, BRIGHT EYES, AIR, PHOENIX.

WHAT IS THIS? AN **"INTRO TO EARLY 2000S INDIE ROCK"** COMPILATION?

MAYBE ON THE WAY BACK, DUDE.

YEAH, OKAY.

WHY ARE YOU SUCH A **DICK**, CAMERON?

I DON'T KNOW. BECAUSE IT'S FUNNY?

IT IS PRETTY FUNNY.

ANYWAY, I'M **NOT** A DICK!

I'M DRIVING YOU GUYS TO THE CITY TO SEE A BAND. I CAN SAY WHATEVER I WANT. YOU GUYS **OWE** ME.

IT'S NOT MY FAULT HE HAS NO SENSE OF HUMOR.

NO, DUDE! YOU ALWAYS PULL THIS KIND OF STUFF AND IT'S NOT COOL!

IT'S JUST A JOKE, JAKE. DON'T WORRY ABOUT IT.

IT'S JUST CAMERON'S SENSE OF HUMOR.

IT'S FINE.

HA HA HA HA

SEE?

OH MY GOD, ARI.

TOSS

NO BIG DEAL.

TRIP MIX

CHK

THIS BAND IS SO GOOD.

YEAH! I CAN'T WAIT TILL WE MOVE OUT HERE AND WE CAN GO SEE BANDS LIKE THIS ALL THE TIME.

WE ARE GOING TO **BE** A BAND LIKE THIS!

I STILL CAN'T BELIEVE YOUR DAD IS LETTING YOU LEAVE WHEN YOUR SISTER JUST LEFT.

THAT'S VERY COOL OF HIM.

YEAH. I DON'T KNOW. WE'LL SEE.

IS MARIA GONNA BE COMING BACK TO VISIT ANYTIME SOON?

WHAT?!

NOTHING. NEVER MIND.

WHAT ARE YOU IDIOTS TALKING ABOUT?

UGH.

ARI'S DAD WANTS HIM TO WORK AT THE BAKERY FOREVER UNTIL HE DIES!

HA

HA HA

WELL, SCREW THAT, MAN! YOU GOTTA COME WITH US. SCREW YOUR DAD. WHO CARES WHAT HE WANTS.

YOU'VE GOTTA LIVE YOUR OWN LIFE.

YEAH!

HEY. I HAVE A WEIRD QUESTION.

DO YOU **LIKE** CAMERON?

WHAT, LIKE, **LIKE** LIKE HIM?

EW. NO.

I MEAN, DO YOU LIKE HIM AS A PERSON.

I HATE HOW ARI LOOKS UP TO HIM. IT'S GROSS.

I GUESS I NEVER REALLY THOUGHT ABOUT IT. HE'S JUST...

...CAMERON.

LIKE, **LOOK AT THAT!**

HAHA

HA HA

THAT'S JUST THEIR...DYNAMIC, OR WHATEVER.

DON'T WORRY ABOUT IT. LET'S HAVE A FUN WEEKEND!

WHAT ARE YOU—

I AM THE JAKE-BOT. I AM CAPABLE OF...FUN.

HA HAA

WHAT IS LOVE? *BZZZT* WHAT IS LOVE? *BZZZT* WHAT IS *BZZZT* LOOOOOOVE?

IS THE JOB STILL AVAILABLE?

THAT DEPENDS.

WHY DO YOU WANT TO WORK IN A BAKERY?

IT'S WHAT I'M GOING TO SCHOOL FOR.

WAIT. REALLY? FOR BAKING?

I JUST FINISHED MY FIRST YEAR AT CULINARY SCHOOL, BUT I THINK I NEED TO TAKE A YEAR OFF...

...FOR FAMILY STUFF.

rub rub

HONESTLY, YOU'RE THE FIRST NON-CRAZY PERSON WHO HAS APPLIED FOR THIS JOB, SO WHY DON'T YOU COME BACK TOMORROW AND WE'LL SEE HOW IT GOES.

HECTORRRR!

WE'VE MISSED YOU SO MUCH, LITTLE BUD.

WHEN ARE YOU COMING BACK TO BIRMINGHAM?

WELL, I DON'T THINK I'M GOING TO MAKE IT BY THE FALL, SO...I GUESS...AFTER CHRISTMAS, MAYBE.

IT MIGHT EVEN BE START OF NEXT YEAR.

NEXT YEAR?!

YOU NEED A LITTLE HELP, MEG?

YES!

HELP IS ON THE WAY, BABE.

I'M JUST GOING TO MONITOR THE SITUATION FROM THIS COMFY COUCH.

WANT A BOOST?

YES, PLEASE.

OH!

HECTOR! IF YOU HAVE SPECIAL FEELINGS FOR ME, YOU CAN JUST LET ME KNOW, YOU KNOW?

haha

SORRY!

GOT 'EM!

NO NO, IT'S FINE. I LIKED IT.

MAYBE A LITTLE TOO MUCH.

EW! GET A ROOM!

HECTOR! COME SIT!

IT'S, LIKE, IMPOSSIBLE FOR HIM TO GO IN A KITCHEN AND NOT BAKE SOMETHING.

HE'S LIKE SOME KIND OF ANCIENT WARRIOR!

"I CANNOT SHEATH MY SPATULA UNTIL IT HAS SPREAD FROSTING."

FINE! FINE!

HA HA HA HA

I MADE SOMETHING EARLIER ANYWAY.

OF **COURSE** YOU DID.

TA-DA!

WHOA, MAN! LOOK AT THIS THING!

DID YOU MAKE ALL OF THESE LITTLE CARROTS?!

THEY'RE SO CUTE!

YUMMM!

THIS IS SO GOOD, HECTOR.

YOU NEED TO COME BACK DOWN SOUTH AND START BAKING US FOOD AGAIN.

LIKE... SOONER THAN NEXT YEAR.

I KNOW YOU HAVE TO HANDLE STUFF WITH YOUR NANA'S HOUSE, BUT WHAT ABOUT **YOUR** LIFE?

IT'S TRUE.

I REALLY MISS YOU COOKING FOR ME ALL THE TIME.

GOD, ANDREW.

YOU REALLY MISS HECTOR DOING **EVERYTHING** FOR YOU ALL THE TIME.

RUDE!

IT'S TRUE, THOUGH, HECTOR.

EVERYBODY MISSES YOU.

AWWW!

I MISS YOU GUYS, TOO.

IT'S ACTUALLY KIND OF STRANGE BEING OUT HERE AT NANA'S HOUSE BY MYSELF.

IT'S ONLY BEEN A COUPLE MONTHS SINCE SHE PASSED, BUT BEING HERE...IT FEELS LIKE I'M WITH HER EVERY DAY.

I KNOW IT SOUNDS SAD, BUT IT'S NICE.

I THINK I NEEDED THIS TIME FOR MYSELF, TOO.

IT'S NICE TO BE ALONE FOR A BIT.

I'M SITTING RIGHT HERE, YOU KNOW!

AHah haha

YOU GUYS WANT COFFEE?

OH, GOD, NO.

I'M GONNA GO TO SLEEP, FELLAS.

HAVE FUN WITH YOUR 11 PM COFFEE.

Smek

IT'S GOOD TO SEE YOU, SWEETIE.

DON'T KEEP HIM UP TOO LATE.

I NEED HIM TO HELP ME DRIVE BACK TOMORROW.

OKAY. I LOVE YOU, MEG.

LOVE BOTH OF YOU! GOOD NIGHT!

GOOD NIGHT, EGG!

YOU WANNA WATCH SOMETHING?

GILMORE GIRLS?

YES, PLEASE.

SHIFT

HA HA HA

THIS IS NICE. LIKE OLD TIMES.

YEAH, IT IS.

WHOA!

HEY,
HECTOR.

HEY, ARI!
HOW'S IT
GOIN'?

BORED.

IT'S SO
SLOOOOW
IN HERE
TODAY.

WELL, LET'S DO
SOMETHING! IT'S MY
FIRST DAY. I'M READY
TO GET TO WORK.
SHOW ME STUFF!

OKAY.

SURE.

SO, WHAT'S
THE PLAN?

WE BAKE ALL THE BAGUETTES FOR THE FRENCH RESTAURANT DOWN THE STREET, SO WE'VE GOTTA BAKE LIKE FOUR DOZEN OF THOSE TODAY.

SOUNDS PERFECT!

DOES ONE OF US NOT NEED TO STAY OUT FRONT?

NO WAY. NOBODY COMES IN HERE, LIKE, EVER. WE MOSTLY DO DELIVERIES.

OHHHHH, OKAY.

LET'S SEE...

WE'VE GOT THE PREP AREA HERE.

A BIG OL' MIXER.

ALL THE SUPPLIES LIKE FLOUR AND OIL ARE DOWN HERE.

AND THE OVENS.

ONE OF THE KNOBS ON THIS THING IS KINDA MESSED UP,

SO YOU HAVE TO FIDDLE WITH IT TO TURN IT OFF SOMETIMES.

SO ARE WE NOT MAKING BAGUETTES?

NO. I MEAN... *YES*, WE ARE. WE JUST HAVE TO DO IT *RIGHT*.

MY DAD JUST LIKES THINGS DONE A CERTAIN WAY. HE'S BEEN USING THE SAME RECIPES FOR TWENTY YEARS.

"EVER SINCE I WAS A YOUNG MAN BACK IN GREECE!"

ANYWAY, THE DOUGH HAS ALREADY BEEN RISING OVERNIGHT. WE JUST HAVE TO DO THE SHAPING AND BAKING TODAY.

WELL, *YOU* DO. I'M JUST GONNA WATCH AND SEE HOW YOU DO.

JUST FOLLOW THE INSTRUCTIONS AND YOU SHOULD BE FINE.

WHUMP

WHUMP

Sliiide

...OH, IS THE BIG DUMB BOY SCOUT HELPING YOU TODAY?...

HAHAHA

SHUT UP, CAMERON. HE'S RIGHT BACK THERE.

HAHAHA

WHAT?! *YOU'RE* THE ONE WHO SAID IT!

HAHA

HEY, HECTOR!

OH MY GOD. STOP.

HAHAHA

I'LL SEE YOU GUYS TONIGHT FOR PRACTICE?

SURE.

YESS!

BYEEE, HECTOR!

DUDE, STOP!

GET OUT!

HA HA HA HA

YEAH... SO 15 OR 20 MINUTES TO RISE AND THEN—

YEAH. I THINK IT'S BEEN LONG ENOUGH. I'M GONNA GO GET THESE IN THE OVEN.

OKAY. SOUNDS GOOD...

SIGH

IT'S ALL ABOUT MAXIMIZING TICKET RETURN, JAKE.

EVERY BALL I STICK IN THIS LITTLE HOLE BRINGS ME ONE STEP CLOSER TO HAVING **ALL THE TICKETS.**

BUT THE TICKETS ARE WORTHLESS. ALL THE PRIZES ARE JUST JUNK.

IT'S NOT ABOUT THE PRIZES, MAN. IT'S ABOUT THE TICKETS.

I HAVE THE MOST TICKETS...

...THEREFORE, I AM THE MOST BEST.

IT'S **MATH,** DUDE.

OKAY, PROFESSOR HANNA.

SMAK

I CAN'T WAIT TO SQUIRREL AWAY ALL OF THESE TICKETS.

I AM A VERY MISERLY PERSON, YOU KNOW.

OH NO.

OH NONO NONO.

WHAT ARE YOU "OH NO"-ING ABOUT?

LOOK.

LOOOOOOOK.

OOH, CUTE!

THAT IS NOT CUTE, HANNA.

WE'RE TRYING TO MOVE OUT OF THIS TOWN AND WE'RE COUNTING ON **THESE TWO** TO HELP MAKE THAT HAPPEN.

THE **LAST THING** WE NEED IS FOR THEM TO FALL IN LOVE.

WHO'S IN LOVE?

EEP!

OH, HEY, ARI.

IT'S LAUREN AND CAMERON.

LOOK.

EHE. HEHE.

NOD NOD

THAT DOESN'T MEAN THEY'RE IN LOVE. THEY'RE JUST...

...BEING FRIENDLY.

I DON'T SEE WHY IT'S ANY OF OUR BUSINESS, ANYWAY.

NONE OF OUR BUSINESS??

WE COULD HAVE A REAL YOKO ONO-TYPE SITUATION ON OUR HANDS.

THAT'S SEXIST, JAKE.

I'M NOT SAYING LAUREN IS YOKO! MAYBE CAMERON IS YOKO!

ALL I'M SAYING IS... SOMEONE IS YOKO.

I ACTUALLY LIKE YOKO.

YEAH. YOKO IS COOL.

ARI! BUDDY!

YOU'RE HERE!

YOU GUYS WERE KIND OF DICKS TO HECTOR AT THE BAKERY.

WHAT?! I DIDN'T SAY ANYTHING!

OKAY. WELL I GUESS JUST...

...CAMERON WAS KIND OF A DICK.

YEAH. THAT SEEMS MORE LIKELY.

SO JUST CHILL WITH THAT, OKAY?

WHY DO YOU CARE, ARI?

ARE YOU IN **LOVE** WITH HIM OR SOMETHING?

NO!

I JUST NEED HIM TO WORK OUT AT THE BAKERY, AND HE'S NOT GONNA STICK AROUND IF YOU GUYS ARE JERKS TO HIM.

AGAIN.

WASN'T ME.

ALSO, ARI...TO BE FAIR...YOU WERE LAUGHING ALONG WITH EVERYBODY ELSE.

WELL, WHOEVER IT WAS, JUST TAKE IT DOWN A NOTCH, PLEASE.

YEAH, SURE.

WHATEVER, DUDE.

WRRRRRRRRR

HECTOR...

WHAT ARE YOU DOING...

IT'S LIKE...

IT'S 11 AM!

I CAN'T BELIEVE MY DAD LET ME SLEEP THIS LATE.

NIKOS LET ME IN THIS MORNING AND THEN LEFT WITH YOUR MOM.

WRRRRR

ANNNNND...

PAP

...YOU'RE DONE.

HE SAID THEY WERE GOING OUT ON THE TOWN TOGETHER.

ALONE.

AND HE SAID WE "CAN HANDLE IT" AND THAT WE "BETTER HANDLE IT."

THAT'S WEIRD. THEY NEVER DO...ANYTHING.

WELL, THEY WERE DRESSED UP CUTE.

IT WAS—

UNF

—ADORABLE.

CAN YOU SHOW ME WHERE THE MUFFIN TINS ARE?

OH! YEAH! I'LL GRAB THEM.

WHAT KIND OF MUFFINS ARE YOU MAKING?

BLUEBERRY!

I'M MAKING THE STREUSEL NOW.

3 TBSP FLOUR

3/4 CUP SUGAR

BUTTER

1/3 CUP OF MELTED BUTTER

CINNAMON

1/4 TEASPOON CINNAMON

THESE TURNED OUT BEAUTIFUL!

LOOK AT THAT.

YOU REALLY LOVE IT.

LOVE WHAT? THIS MUFFIN?

NO!

BAKING.

OH, YEAH.

I REALLY DO.

IS ARI HERE?

I THINK HE'S IN THE SHOWER.

WELL, WE SHOULD TALK TO HIM ABOUT IT WHEN HE GETS OUT.

NOT TONIGHT.

I JUST WANT TO GO TO SLEEP.

OKAY, BUT—

WE'LL TELL HIM SOON.

OKAY.

ARI, WE'RE HOME!

I'M IN THE SHOWER!

OKAY. WE'RE GOING TO BED.

TALK TO YOU IN THE MORNING, HONEY. LOVE YOU.

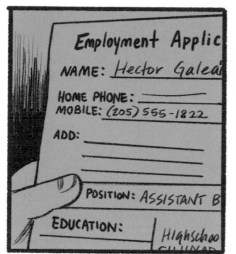

Employment Applic

NAME: _Hector Galeai_

HOME PHONE: _____
MOBILE: (205) 555-1822

ADD: _____
_____
_____

POSITION: ASSISTANT B

EDUCATION: | Highschoo

Hey Hector.
It's Ari.

July

IT'S ALWAYS LIKE THIS ON FOURTH OF JULY.

EAST BEACH GETS FLOODED WITH TOURISTS.

AND THEY ALL COME IN FOR THE *Kyrkos Family Bakery's Famous* ✧ *Sourdough Rolls!* ✧

Sourdough Rolls

IT SAYS FAMOUS RIGHT IN THE NAME!

I DON'T THINK THAT'S HOW IT WORKS.

HA

Ahaha

ding
ding

WE'RE BACK!

HAPPY INDEPENDENCE DAY!

FINALLY!

WHAT DO YOU MEAN, "FINALLY"?

WE WERE GETTING PAPER FOR THE CASH REGISTER.

DON'T BE RUDE.

BUT IT'S THE BUSIEST DAY OF THE YEAR—!

WHICH IS **WHY** WE HAD TO GO GET **PAPER!**

IT'S FINE, ARI. DON'T WORRY ABOUT IT SO MUCH.

LISTEN TO HECTOR, ARI!

HE'S A GOOD KID.

THIS STUPID THING!!

CLACK

HERE. LET ME DO IT.

GOT IT!

AND SORRY, DAD. I DON'T EVEN KNOW WHY I FLIPPED OUT.

IT'S OKAY.

OKAY, NOW. WHO IS NEXT?

WHO WANTS SOME FAMOUS SOURDOUGH ROLLS?

ding

Sorry WE'RE Closed

DID WE HAVE A GOOD DAY?

OF COURSE!

FOURTH OF JULY IS ALWAYS GOOD FOR US.

IT'S VERY FORTUNATE TIMING, TOO.

WE NEEDED THIS.

WELL, I THINK ME AND HECTOR ARE GOING TO GO GET SOME FOOD.

HEY, CAN I TAKE A LITTLE OF THIS STARTER? I WANNA MAKE SOME FAMOUS ROLLS AT HOME!

Tappa

Tappa *Tappa*

OF COURSE, HECTOR!

YOU GUYS WANNA JOIN US FOR DINNER?

HEH?

HEH?

Ha Ha Ha

NO, YOU GUYS GO HAVE FUN. YOUR DAD AND I WILL CLOSE UP.

...AND I HOPE YOU HAVE A *ROCKIN'* GOOD MEAL TONIGHT HERE AT THE *DINNERETTE.*

ppthp

HEY, THERE, COOL CATS! WELCOME TO THE DINN—

OH MY GOD! ARI!

YOU'RE HERE TO SAVE ME!

Ha Ha Ha

NOT REALLY. WE'RE JUST HERE FOR DINNER.

OOOOH! IS THIS HECTOR?

HI.

HANNA. NICE TO MEET YOU.

WE KIND OF MET ALREADY. WHEN YOU CAME INTO THE BAKERY WITH JAKE AND CAMERON.

OH. I DIDN'T KNOW YOU COULD HEAR US.

heh heh

CAMERON CAN BE KIND OF...INSENSITIVE SOMETIMES.

ANYWAY! HOPEFULLY THAT'S ALL WATER UNDER THE BRIDGE...

please wa

...AND YOU CAN HAVE A ROCKIN' GOOD MEAL TONIGHT HERE AT THE DINNERETTE!

menu

menu

AHHH! ARI! I CAN'T BELIEVE YOU CAME TO VISIT ME AT WORK!

123

OKAY! I'LL BE BACK WITH YOU SHORTLY! BYEEE!

BYEEE.

UGH. HANNA IS THE BEST.

MHM.

HEY. WHY ARE YOU MAD?

...

I'M NOT MAD. YOUR FRIENDS WERE JUST RUDE TO ME. THAT'S ALL.

I DIDN'T LIKE IT.

NAHHH.

ANYWAY, SHE SAID SHE WAS SORRY!

WHAT?

NO, SHE DIDN'T.

SHE **VERY** QUICKLY CHANGED THE SUBJECT.

WELL, I'M SURE SHE **MEANT** TO SAY SHE WAS SORRY.

OH MY GOD, ARI.

JUST FORGET I SAID ANYTHING.

BUT—

DROP IT.

AND A 100% PAID FOR SODA FOR YOU, SIR!

VERY SLICK.

SEE! SHE BROUGHT YOU A SODA!

REALLY?!

WAIT, WHAT HAPPENED?

NOTHING. IT'S JUST—

OH NO.

I GOTTA GET OUT OF HERE.

WHY?

IT'S THAT LADY, DEB. SHE WAS VERY...FORWARD WITH ME THE OTHER DAY.

FORWARD?

OOOH, IS THAT HER IN THE LEOPARD PRINT?!

YES! NOW HUSH. SHE'S GONNA HEAR YOU.

WHAT DID SHE DO?

SHE WANTS TO MAKE OUT WITH ME. SHE KNEW MY DAD. SHE'S...

...TERRIFYING.

UMMMM...?

HECTOR'S STALKER IS HERE. WE NEED TO MAKE AN EXIT!

DO YOU WANT ME TO CAUSE A DISTRACTION?

THAT WOULD BE AMAZING.

OKAY.

I'M ON IT.

HULLABALOO!

HULLABALOO!

HULLABALOO!

HA HA HA

Hah
Hah
Hah
Hah

HAH

HF

DO YOU THINK WE LOST HER?

huff huff

MHM. YEAH. PROBABLY.

BUT NOW WE HAVE TO GO BACK.

NOT YET. COME ON.

UP
HERE.

UNF.

I'M
HERE!

WHERE IS
HERE?

PUSH

LOOK.

SWEEE

ARISTOTLE!

WHAT!

YOU TAKE TOO LONG WITH YOUR PART.

Hmph

HERE. LET ME SHO—

OH, GOODNESS.

YOU NEED TO CALM DOWN, BOY.

NOW, LOOK...

IT'S EASY.

SEE?

AYYYYY!

SEE, WHAT DID I TELL YOU?

A GOOD BOY!

SMEK

ACK!!

YOU HELP ARI ROLL THE DOUGH.

HE CAN'T KEEP UP WITH ME!

OH MY GOD.

HA HA HA HA

HE'S DRIVING ME CRAZY TODAY.

WHO?

YOUR DAD?

YES!

AWW, WHY?

I LIKE HIM.

HE'S SO HAPPY. JUST LOOK AT HIM.

♪

OF COURSE **YOU** LIKE HIM.

YOU LIKE **EVERYBODY.**

AND ALSO... HE'S NOT **YOUR** DAD.

HEY!

I DON'T LIKE **EVERYBODY.**

HE AND YOUR MOM ARE JUST BOTH SO CUTE AND SWEET.

I ENVY THEM.

WHERE **IS** YOUR MOM, ANYWAY?

HEY. WHY ISN'T MOM HELPING US?

DON'T WE HAVE, LIKE, A MILLION LOAVES OF BREAD TO GET READY BEFORE THE FAIR TOMORROW?

YOUR MOTHER IS WORKING ON FINANCES.

WHY? IS THIS TOO MUCH WORK FOR YOU?

NO!

I WAS JUST ASKING.

WELL, WE TALKED ABOUT THIS ALREADY, ARI.

THE BAKERY ISN'T DOING GOOD. YOUR MOTHER IS TRYING TO FIGURE OUT HOW TO MAKE THE MONEY WORK.

I DON'T KNOW WHY I HAVE TO TELL YOU EVERYTHING ONE HUNDRED TIMES BEFORE YOU UNDERSTAND.

LOOK. I'M GOING TO LET THIS BATCH RISE AND COME BACK DOWN IN A BIT.

I NEED A BREAK.

SORRY, DAD. I WAS JUST ASKING WHERE MOM WAS.

NO. IT'S FINE.

JUST FINISH UP ROLLING THAT BATCH AND THEN COME GET ME AND WE'LL FINISH ALL THIS.

YOU'RE A GOOD BOY, TOO, ARI.

EVEN IF YOUR HEAD IS A LITTLE THICK.

HE HAS A POINT.

WHAT?

YOUR HEAD **IS** A LITTLE THICK.

JUST...ROLL THE THINGS.

JEEZ.

WELL, WE DID IT!

JUST LOOK AT THAT.

NOW, AS LONG AS YOU CAN SELL A LOT TOMORROW, WE MIGHT NOT GO OUT OF BUSINESS!

I'M SURE WE'LL SELL ALL OF IT!

HOW COULD WE NOT?

IT'S ALL SO GLORIOUS.

LET'S GET THIS VAN LOADED NOW.

YOU TWO HAVE AN EARLY DRIVE TO THE FAIR TOMORROW AND IT'S ALREADY LATE.

WHAT TIME IS IT, ANYWAY?

Cameron 11:25 AM
GOIN TO CHECK OUT PLACES IN THE CITY TODAY, U WANNA COME

OH NO!

WHAT HAPPENED?

NOTHING!

IT'S JUST ALREADY EIGHT O'CLOCK!

LET'S GET THIS VAN LOADED UP FOR TOMORROW!

OKAY! YOU GUYS ALL SET FOR TOMORROW?

GOT EVERYTHING?

YEP.

YEP.

GO TO SLEEP, THEN!

IT WILL BE 4 AM BEFORE YOU KNOW IT!

FOUR

A

M

WHAT HELL...

IS THIS...?

HA HA HA

YOU'LL WAKE UP SOON.

WE'VE STILL GOT ANOTHER HOUR OR SO UNTIL WE GET TO THE FAIR, ANYWAY.

YOU COULD JUST TRY TO GO BACK TO SLEEP.

NO. IT'S OKAY. I'LL KEEP YOU COMPANY.

WHERE ARE WE?

WE JUST PASSED MILLERSVILLE.

MAYBE TEN MINUTES AGO?

SO MANY
TREES...

WHAT
WAS
THAT?

DID
YOU HIT
SOMETHING?

DUDE! I
DON'T KNOW!
CALM DOWN!

WATCH
OUT!!

LET
GO!!

NO.

I SAVED US.

YOU DIDN'T EVEN SEE THAT DEER.

CHK-RRRRR

OKAY, ARI.

JUST GIVE ME FIVE MINUTES AND I'LL HAVE US BACK ON THE ROAD.

I'M NOT GETTING ANY SIGNAL.

WHY DO YOU NEED A SIGNAL?

I JUST DO, OKAY? THIS IS HOW A LOT OF HORROR MOVIES START, YOU KNOW?

I'VE NEVER SEEN A HORROR MOVIE THAT STARTS AT 5 AM.

WELL...

...THERE'S A FIRST TIME FOR EVERYTHING.

Clang

CAN YOU ROLL ME THAT TIRE?

HUH?

OH, YEAH.

MARYLAN
FAIR GROU
NEXT EXI

CHAD?!

HECTOR?

WHAT ARE YOU **DOING** HERE?

I HONESTLY THOUGHT I WOULD NEVER SEE YOU AGAIN AFTER YOU DROPPED OUT.

YEAH, MAN. THE ACADEMY WASN'T FOR ME, DUDE.

I STILL LOVE COOKING, THOUGH! I JUST WANTED TO GET OUT AND DO MY OWN THING.

I'M NOT REALLY A SCHOOL KINDA GUY.

BUT NOW I'M OUT ON THE ROAD, MAN.

I LOVE IT!

WHOA. YOU'RE WORKING FOR THE FAIR?

YEAH!

OR NOT THE FAIR, BUT JUST ALL OVER.

I WORK FOR A COMPANY THAT PROVIDES RIDES FOR DIFFERENT FAIRS AND EVENTS AND STUFF.

ENOUGH ABOUT ME, THOUGH, MAN.

HOW ARE YOU?

HOW'S ANDREW?

OH, ANDREW AND I BROKE UP.

AW, MAN. HECTOR, MY DUDE.

I THOUGHT YOU GUYS WERE LIFERS.

YOU DOING OKAY?

YEAH. I'M OKAY.

IT WAS ROUGH FOR A LITTLE WHILE, BUT YEAH...I'M FINE NOW.

WELL, HEY! I HAVE TO FINISH SETTING UP. COME FIND ME LATER, THOUGH?

WE'LL CATCH UP!

SOUNDS GOOD, MAN!

SEE YA!

WHO WAS THAT?

...HUH? YOU MEAN CHAD?

I DUNNO.

DID YOU NOT JUST HEAR ME YELL "CHAD?!" REALLY LOUD?

OHHHH... "CHAD."

DID YOU TELL HIM I SAVED YOUR LIFE THIS MORNING?

WHUMP

HEY!

THANKS, MA'AM.

I'LL TAKE TEN BREADS, PLEASE!

JAKE!!!

AHHH! WATCH OUT, BUDDY.

YOU'RE GONNA SQUISH THE MERCHANDISE.

I'M GLAD TO SEE YOU!

ME AND HECTOR ARE ABOUT TO BE DONE FOR THE DAY.

YOU WANNA HANG OUT AND DO FAIR STUFF?

YES!

I AM AT THE FAIR SPECIFICALLY TO DO FAIR STUFF.

AND TO SEE YOU, OF COURSE.

I BROUGHT THE WHOLE GANG!

AH, COOOOL.

IT WAS TOTALLY HANNA'S IDEA.

SHE WANTED TO SURPRISE YOU.

HANNA, I LOVE YOU!

I LOVE YOU, ARI!!

OKAY. GIVE ME A FEW MINUTES TO PACK ALL THIS UP AND THEN WE CAN *HANG.*

IT'S ALL PACKED UP ALREADY!

WE SOLD ALMOST EVERYTHING!

YOUR DAD IS GOING TO BE PRETTY HAPPY.

HECTOR. NICE TO MEET YOU.

JAKE.

YOU WANNA HANG WITH US AND EAT SOME FUNNEL CAKES?

YES!

SO ARE YOU GUYS, LIKE, AN OFFICIAL THING NOW?

YES, ARI. WE'RE AN "OFFICIAL" THING.

BUT I DON'T KNOW WHY YOU NEED TO PUT EVERYTHING IN A BOX.

WE'VE BEEN LOOKING FOR A PLACE TOGETHER IN BALTIMORE.

THE SCENE IS SO MUCH BETTER FOR BANDS THERE.

WAIT.

I THOUGHT WE WERE ALL LOOKING FOR A PLACE TOGETHER.

YEAH, MAN. SURE.

WE CAN DO THAT STILL. IT'S NOT LIKE YOU'VE BEEN REALLY HELPING US FIND AN APARTMENT, THOUGH.

I JUST ASSUMED YOU WEREN'T INTERESTED ANYMORE.

WHAT! OF COURSE I'M INTERESTED!

I'VE JUST BEEN BUSY WITH THE BAKERY.

BUT THAT'S TEMPORARY. AFTER THIS SUMMER, I'M DONE WITH BAKING.

IT'S COOL, ARI.

YOU DON'T NEED TO PROVE ANYTHING TO ME.

LET'S GO PLAY SOME GAMES.

YASSSSS.

TAKE ME TO THE GAME WITH THE MOST TICKETS!!

BYEEE!!

SEE YOU GUYS LATER EVEN THOUGH WE ARE GOING TO THE SAME PLACE!

LET'S ALL HANG OUT SOON!

THAT WAS FUN!

SEE, MY FRIENDS AREN'T SO BAD!

I NEVER SAID THEY WERE BAD, ARI.

BUT, YEAH. I HAD FUN TODAY.

HANGING OUT WITH YOUR FRIENDS AND WORKING THE BOOTH WITH YOU.

I THINK WE MAKE A GOOD TEAM.

YAWWWN

YOU CAN GO TO SLEEP IF YOU WANT. I'LL WAKE YOU UP WHEN WE GET CLOSE TO HOME.

NO...

IT'S OKAY...

I'LL KEEP YOU...

...COMPANY...

179

WHAT ABOUT MY FACE?

RAAARGH!

OKAY, OKAY. WE SHOULD STOP.

ARI!

OH, NO.

WHAT IS THIS MESS?

THESE INGREDIENTS COST MONEY, YOU KNOW.

I'M SORRY, MOM.

HECTOR AND I WERE JUST MESSING AROUND.

IT WON'T HAPPEN AGAIN.

SORRY, MRS. KYRKOS.

I'M GLAD YOU TWO ARE HAVING FUN, BUT WE HAVE TO BE CAREFUL WITH MONEY RIGHT NOW.

BUT WE DID GOOD AT THE STATE FAIR, RIGHT? WE SOLD ALMOST EVERYTHING.

IT'S TRUE. IT WAS GOOD. AND THAT'S WHY WE'RE STILL OPEN.

JUST... BE MORE MINDFUL.

OKAY?

YEAH! OF COURSE!

DEFINITELY.

NOW FINISH UP THOSE RED VELVET CUPCAKES.

AND SAVE A COUPLE FOR YOUR MOM, WILL YA?

CREAK

CREAK

CREAK

CREAK SHUT

he he.

flick

OKAY!

I STILL NEEEED...

SEVEN CUPS OF FLOUR.

GOT IT!

OKAY, AND THREE CUPS OF MILK.

SHHHK

GOT IT!

THOSE ARE SOME NICE *Red Velvet Cupcakes.*

NOW I'VE JUST GOTTA RUN THESE THINGS DOWN TO THE PARK.

I'LL GO WITH YOU.

YOU SURE? YOUR SHIFT IS OVER, BUDDY. YOU DON'T ACTUALLY HAVE TO DO ANY MORE WORK TODAY.

I KNOW, BUT I DON'T HAVE ANYTHING ELSE TO DO, TO BE HONEST.

ha ha

WORKS FOR ME.

I DIDN'T WANT TO CARRY THAT OH-SO-HEAVY TRAY OF CUPCAKES ANYWAY.

I NEED A BIG STRONG **MAN** TO HELP ME.

PAP

OKAY. I'M LEAVING NOW.

HA HA

WAIT FOR ME!

I THINK HANNA AND JAKE ARE GONNA BE AT THIS **SCREEN ON THE GREEN** THING TONIGHT.

HANNA WILL BE HAPPY TO SEE YOU. I THINK SHE'S IN LOVE WITH YOU.

HEH, WELL... I DON'T THINK THAT'S GOING TO WORK OUT, UNFORTUNATELY.

HA HA

Kyrko Famil Baker

DID YOU SEE HIM?

...THE CAPTAIN PLANET GUY...

ARE YOU GUYS READY FOR THIS MOVIE??

I DON'T EVEN KNOW WHAT MOVIE IS PLAYING.

NIGHT OF THE COMET!

NEVER HEARD OF IT.

YEAH. ME, EITHER.

ME, EITHER.

WHAT?!

OKAY! IT'S THESE TWO SISTERS AND THE WORLD ENDS AND THERE IS THIS RED MIST THAT APPEARS EVERYWHERE AND EVERYONE IS TURNED INTO PILES OF DUST.

HE GETS LIKE THIS SOMETIMES.

YEAH. IT'S BEST TO JUST NOD AND LOOK EXCITED.

MHM! YAS BUDDY YAS.

AND ANYWAY...I DON'T WANT TO SPOIL IT FOR YOU. IT'S ABOUT TO START!

I STILL CAN'T BELIEVE YOU WON THE RAFFLE.

"48 RED VELVET CUPCAKES FROM KYRKOS FAMILY BAKERY!"

ha ha ha

WHAT CAN I SAY? I'M A VERY LUCKY GUY.

KYRKOS FAMILY BA

WELL. THIS IS YOU.

YEAH, I GUESS SO.

UNLESS...

WE COULD KEEP HANGING OUT, INSTEAD.

HANG WHERE? IT'S LIKE 12:30.

TRUST ME, MY DEAR HECTOR.

WHERE THERE IS A WILL TO HANG OUT, THERE IS A WAY TO HANG OUT!

GOD, YOU'RE SUCH A DORK.

WHY ARE WE ALWAYS CLIMBING STUFF WHEN WE'RE TOGETHER?

IT'S UNNATURAL.

NO WAY, MAN.

IT'S COOL.

IT'S SO QUIET UP HERE.

IT'S NOT LIKE THE REST OF EAST BEACH IS EXACTLY BUSTLING RIGHT NOW.

THIS IS DIFFERENT, THOUGH. YOU LOOK UP AND THERE'S NOTHING BETWEEN YOU AND THE SKY.

IT'S LIKE YOU COULD BE ANYWHERE IN THE WORLD.

WHY DO YOU WANT TO BE SOMEWHERE ELSE?

HUH?

YOU ALWAYS TALK ABOUT HOW YOU WANT TO MOVE AWAY FROM HERE.

YOU ACT LIKE YOUR LIFE IS SO TERRIBLE.

BUT IT DOESN'T SEEM SO BAD TO ME.

IT'S A BEAUTIFUL TOWN.

YOU'VE GOT FAMILY,

FRIENDS,

A GOOD JOB.

WHAT?

YOU'RE GOOD AT THAT.

MAKING PEOPLE FEEL BETTER.

I KNOW I AM.

IT'S KIND OF AN ISSUE FOR ME.

POOR HECTOR. HE'S SUCH A GOOD GUY.

SHUT UP.

PUSH

HEY! WATCH IT.

I'M TRYING TO HAVE A CHILL TIME OVER HERE.

ARI!

CLAP

BAP

HOLD ON. I'VE GOT YOU.

click

PULL
ME UP!

214

SWOOOP

fssh fssh

WHUMP

Tug
Tug

HEY, HECTOR!

YOU READY TO GET TO WORK?

YEAH, I GUESS.

HEY! YOU WANNA HANG OUT WITH SOME OF MY FRIENDS TONIGHT? THEY'RE IN TOWN FOR A DAY.

SURE!

IT'S BEAUTIFUL.

WHAT?

THE PHYLLO?

YEAH.

THEY'RE SO IN SYNC.

IT'S SO COOL.

THEY'VE BEEN MAKING PHYLLO LIKE THAT SINCE I WAS A KID.

THEY USE IT FOR BAKLAVA FOR THE STORE, BUT MY MOM MAKES SPANAKOPITA WITH IT, TOO.

I'LL BRING YOU SOME THE NEXT TIME SHE MAKES IT.

Sorry WE'RE closed

YES, PLEASE.

IT'S SOOOO GOOOOD.

CLOSE YOUR MOUTH. YOU'RE DROOLING ALL OVER THE REGISTER.

I WOULD LOVE TO HAVE SOMETHING LIKE THAT...

TO BE ON A TEAM WITH SOMEONE...

...AND TO BE BETTER TOGETHER THAN YOU EVER COULD BE ALONE.

IT'S SO SWEET. DON'T YOU THINK?

YEAH.

IT IS.

DING DING

CLAP

WELP! LET'S SELL SOME BAKED GOODS!

HOW HAVE I NEVER EVEN HEARD OF THIS PLACE?

EAST BEACH ISN'T THAT BIG.

THAT'S MEG FOR YOU.

HA HA

SHE FOUND IT ONLINE.

I THINK THEY OPENED, LIKE, YESTERDAY.

WHO'S THAT WITH HER?

THAT'S ANDREW.

LIKE...*ANDREW*, ANDREW?

OH MY GOD, ARI. DON'T MAKE A BIG DEAL OUT OF IT, PLEASE.

ARI!

I'VE HEARD SO MUCH ABOUT YOU!

REALLY?

YES!

HECTOR NEVER STOPS TALKING ABOUT YOU AND THE BAKERY AND YOUR CUTE FAMILY.

MEG IS A HUGGER.

IT'S JUST MY NATURAL INSTINCT.

I FEEL LIKE WE ALL KNOW THIS ALREADY, BUT I'M MEG AND THIS IS ANDREW.

HI.

HEY.

BE NICE, ANDREW.

WHAT DID I DO?

HAHA

NOTHING...

...YET.

SO WHAT ARE WE DOING TODAY?

ARI, YOU LIVE HERE. WHAT'S CUTE AND CHEAP TO DO?

WELL, IF YOU GUYS ARE HUNGRY, WE CAN GO DOWN TO THE FISH MARKET.

PERFECT!

THAT WAS DEFINITELY IN MY TOP THREE CHOICES!

I THINK I LIKE YOU, ARISTOTLE!

TO THE FISH MARKET!

DON'T WE HAVE TO PAY?

NOPE. WE DIDN'T ACTUALLY ORDER ANYTHING.

YEAH. I HEARD THE COFFEE IS CRAP, BUT I REALLY WANTED TO SEE THIS CUTE GARDEN PATIO!

THIS IS ADORABLE!

DON'T YOU THINK SO, ANDREW?

HEY!

JAB

YES, MEG. IT'S VERY ADORABLE.

Rub Rub

I DON'T KNOW WHAT'S WRONG WITH HIM.

I THINK HE'S JEALOUS OF YOU.

MEG! YOU NEED TO STOP. I FEEL LIKE YOU'RE BEING VERY IMPISH RIGHT NOW.

WHO? ME?!

YES! THAT'S EXACTLY THE TYPE OF THING THAT AN IMPISH PERSON WOULD SAY.

Ha Ha Ha

SO, ARI! HECTOR TELLS ME YOU'RE IN A BAND! WHAT KIND OF MUSIC IS IT?

IT'S, LIKE... INDIE POP STUFF.

KIND OF LIKE PASSION PIT, MAYBE?

AHHH!

PASSION PIT IS ANDREW'S FAVORITE BAND!

REALLY?

YEAH.

I'VE SEEN THEM PLAY LIKE SIX TIMES.

OH MY GOD. I'M SO JEALOUS.

I'VE NEVER SEEN THEM BEFORE.

YOU SHOULD GO IF YOU CAN!

THE WAY THEY PLAY THEIR SONGS LIVE IS SO DIFFERENT. IT'S REALLY COOL.

I KNOW. I'VE WATCHED LIKE A MILLION VIDEOS ONLINE.

THEY'RE PLAYING HERE IN A COUPLE MO—

LOOK!

YOU GUYS ARE BONDING!

GAH, MEG. YOU'RE SO OVERBEARING SOMETIMES.

I JUST WANT EVERYBODY TO GET ALONG!

EVERYBODY **IS** GETTING ALONG, MEG.

IT'S BEEN FIVE MINUTES.

YOU **HAVE** TO CHILL.

DO YOU GUYS WANT TO EAT?

YES!

THIS PLACE SMELLS HORRIBLE, BUT IT'S ALSO MAKING ME REALLY HUNGRY.

HA HA HA

SO, YOU REALIZE WE'VE NOW COME TO VISIT YOU *TWICE* THIS SUMMER AND YOU HAVEN'T COME TO SEE US AT ALL.

IT'S TRUE.

YOU CAN'T MAKE ME FEEL GUILTY WHEN I'M LITERALLY COMING DOWN TO SEE YOU IN LIKE A WEEK.

YOU ARE?

YEAH! I CLEARED IT WITH YOUR DAD. HE'S GOING TO WORK WHILE I'M GONE.

I'VE BEEN MISSING HOME AND I WANT TO SEE EVERY-BODY.

I CAME STRAIGHT TO NANA'S HOUSE FROM SCHOOL.

I FEEL LIKE I HAVEN'T BEEN HOME IN FOREVER.

GOOD MORNING!

...MORNING...

UMMMM...WHY ARE YOU JUST SITTING IN THE DARK, YOU WEIRDO?

click

UGH.

I'M JUST IN A FOUL MOOD TODAY.

YOU'VE BEEN ACTING LIKE THIS EVER SINCE WE HUNG OUT WITH MEG AND ANDREW THE OTHER DAY.

SNAP OUT OF IT, NOSFERATU.

WE'VE GOT BAGELS TO MAKE.

THMP

WHATEVER.

FINE! I'LL JUST MAKE THEM MYSELF.

DO YOU REALLY HAVE TO GO?

WHAT DO YOU MEAN?

BACK TO BIRMINGHAM?

IS THAT WHAT YOU'RE UPSET ABOUT?

YES! OF COURSE!

I'M GOING TO MISS YOU.

WELL, TO ANSWER YOUR QUESTION, **YES.**

I HAVE TO GO BACK HOME.

I MISS MY FRIENDS. I MISS MY STUFF.

I JUST NEED TO CHECK IN AND MAKE SURE EVERYTHING IS HOW I LEFT IT.

I'LL MISS YOU, TOO, THOUGH.

REALLY?

YES!

IN CASE YOU HAVEN'T NOTICED, WE SPEND A LOT OF TIME TOGETHER, ARI.

IT'S NOT LIKE WE'RE JUST WORK BUDS.

WE HANG OUT EVERY DAY.

YOU'RE BASICALLY MY BEST FRIEND.

OKAY.

AW, WHAT'S WRONG?

NOTHING. NOTHING.

I JUST FEEL THE SAME WAY.

HERE. GIVE ME THAT.

WELL, WHAT DOES THAT MEAN? "NOT REALLY"?

DO YOU MISS HIM?

HUH?

COME HELP ME.

PSSSH

YOU PUNCHED HIM IN THE FACE.

HAHA HA

I DO REMEMBER THAT.

WHY ARE YOU TELLING ME THIS?

I DON'T KNOW. I GUESS YOU'VE JUST ALWAYS BEEN A SENSITIVE BOY.

IT'S NOT A BAD THING, BUT DON'T LET IT RULE YOU, ARI.

THANKS, MOM.

IT'S NO PROBLEM.

I LOVE YOU, MY SWEET BOY.

TA-DA!

OOOOOH. WHAT'S THIS?

IT'S CALLED RAVANI. I LEARNED HOW TO MAKE IT FROM ARI'S MOM.

chomp

IT'S COCONUT CAKE SOAKED IN SYRUP.

IT'S THE MOST SAMOA-Y GREEK FOOD I'VE EVER TASTED.

DUDE!

I WAS GOING TO TRY TO GET YOU TO STAY HERE, BUT NOW I THINK YOU SHOULD GO BACK AND LEARN MORE FOOD LESSONS FROM THIS WOMAN.

THIS IS LIKE CAKE WITCHCRAFT.

I ACTUALLY ALREADY KIND OF MISS THAT LITTLE BAKERY.

IT'S SO WARM AND WELCOMING. I FEEL LIKE I'M PART OF A FAMILY.

YOU MISS YOUR LITTLE BOYFRIEND, IS WHAT YOU MISS.

HE CAN BE A LITTLE SHIT SOMETIMES, BUT FOR SOME REASON I REALLY LIKE BEING AROUND HIM.

HE DID GET A LITTLE WEIRD WHEN I LEFT, THOUGH.

WEIRD HOW?

I DON'T KNOW.

KIND OF CLINGY, I GUESS?

YOU TEND TO HAVE THAT EFFECT ON PEOPLE.

WELL IT'S NOT MY FAULT!

YOU'RE JUST A STUD, STUD.

HAHAHA. I HATE YOU.

ANYWAY, I'M SURE HE'S FINE.

A LITTLE TIME APART IS PROBABLY A GOOD THING FOR HIM.

IT'S NOT THAT BIG OF A DEAL, ARI.

WE BARELY EVER PRACTICED. WE NEVER PLAYED A SHOW.

WE CAN STILL JAM WHENEVER YOU WANT, BUT AS FAR AS THE BAND GOES, LAUREN AND I ARE JUST GOING TO DO OUR OWN THING.

I GET IT.

I JUST HATE IT.

YOU SHOULD LISTEN TO THEM, ARI.

THEY'RE ACTUALLY REALLY GOOD.

WAY BETTER THAN WE EVER WERE, IF I'M BEING HONEST.

THANKS.

THAT DOESN'T MAKE THINGS ANY BETTER!

AND HOW DOES THIS AFFECT OUR PLANS?

WE WERE ALL GOING TO GO GET A PLACE IN BALTIMORE TOGETHER.

NONE OF THAT HAS CHANGED, DUDE.

WE'VE ALL TALKED ABOUT THIS A BUNCH. YOU JUST HAVEN'T BEEN AROUND.

IF YOU THINK ABOUT IT, THIS IS YOUR FAULT, ARI.

CAMERON!

HARSH.

DUDE.

WHAT?

IT'S HARSH, BUT IT'S THE TRUTH.

HEY!
YOU'RE
HERE!

WELL, WELCOME BACK.

HEY. WHAT'S GOING ON?

STOP!

OKAY.

SORRY.

ARE YOU OKAY?

NO!

YOU LEFT ME HERE, HECTOR!

LIKE I JUST DON'T MATTER.

AND I'M OBVIOUSLY NOT IMPORTANT TO MY FRIENDS.

WHAT ARE YOU TALKING ABOUT?

I'M USELESS TO MY FAMILY.

SNRK

I JUST DON'T KNOW WHAT I'M DOING!

ARI. NOBODY KNOWS WHAT THEY'RE DOING.

YOU'RE NOT ALONE IN THAT.

DON'T ACT LIKE YOU UNDERSTAND ME.

IF YOU DID, YOU WOULDN'T HAVE LEFT ME HERE.

LOOK. OBVIOUSLY YOU'RE GOING THROUGH SOMETHING RIGHT NOW, AND YOU'RE TRYING TO PUT IT ON ME.

AND THAT'S NOT GOING TO HAPPEN.

SO I'M GOING TO LEAVE.

OKAY?

CHOP

MORNING.

I'M SORRY ABOUT YESTERDAY. I WAS HAVING A REALLY BAD DAY.

I SHOULDN'T HAVE TREATED YOU LIKE THAT.

I'M AN IDIOT.

I **AM** GLAD YOU'RE BACK, THOUGH.

SQUEEZE

I'M GLAD I'M BACK, TOO.

I'VE GOT BAD NEWS FOR YOU, THOUGH.

YOU'RE WORKING IN THE FRONT TODAY.

TWIRL

PUSH

ARI!
COME HERE!

WHAT?

I'M BAKING
YOU SOMETHING.

YOU'VE BEEN BAKING ALL DAY.

HOW COULD YOU POSSIBLY WANT TO DO MORE?

I GUESS MY SECRET IS FINALLY OUT.

I LOVE BAKING!

WELL, WHAT IS IT?

WHAT, THIS?

THIS IS JUST WHIPPED CREAM.

Ha Ha

HISSS

THUMP

FOOSH

FWOOOSH

HECTOR!

PpCHHHHH

WE CAN PUT IT OUT!

NO, WE CAN'T!

GET OUT NOW!

BEEP
BEEP
BEEP

COUGH

WHAT ARE YOU DOING?! COME ON!

I'M GOING BACK IN!

GRAB

DON'T YOU DARE.

HOW DID THIS HAPPEN?

IT WAS JUST AN ACCID—

IT WAS MY FAULT.

IS THIS TRUE, ARI?

THIS WAS HECTOR'S FAULT?

YES.

I HAVE NO CHOICE, THEN...

...HECTOR, YOU ARE FIRED.

BARK
BARK

Weeeooo

chirp
chirp

SMAK

WAKE UP,
DUDE.

UNGH

YOU GOTTA GET TO WORK, MAN.

IF YOU CAN'T PAY THE RENT, WE'LL HAVE TO GET A NEW ROOMMATE.

I SLEEP ON THE COUCH, CAMERON.

NOBODY ELSE IS GOING TO PAY MONEY TO SLEEP ON YOUR COUCH.

WELL, I DON'T KNOW, MAN.

ALL I'M SAYING IS, YOU PAY THE RENT OR I KICK YOU OUT.

GOT IT?

YEAH. GOT IT.

AND DON'T COME BACK TOO EARLY!

LAUREN AND I NEED TO GET READY FOR OUR SHOW TONIGHT.

SLAM

YOU'RE LATE.

I'M NOT LATE, JULIAN.

WELL, YOU'RE ALMOST LATE.

DON'T BE LATE.

YOU'RE NOT EVEN MY BOSS, JULIAN!

NAH, not really feeling Baltimore tonight.

Come visit us in East Beach, tho we miss you.

YEAH! We miss you! 😭😭

JAKE

HANNA

CHAD?

CHAD!

HEY, MAN!

DO I KNOW YOU?

WE MET ONCE... KINDA.

AT THE STATE FAIR.

I'M HECTOR'S FRIEND.

OH, YEAH! HECTOR, MAN!

I LOVE THAT GUY!

HAVE YOU TALKED TO HIM RECENTLY?

WHO, HECTOR?

NAH, MAN.

I MEAN, HECTOR'S A COOL DUDE, BUT I BARELY KNOW THE GUY.

JUST TEXT HIM OR SOMETHING!

COOL! THANKS, CHAD!

GOOD TO SEE YOU AGAIN!

ziiiiiiip
SHHFF

IT'S GOOD TO SEE YOU, BOY.

YOU WANT SOME FOOD?

HAHA

NO THANKS, DAD. I KNOW IT'S REALLY LATE.

SNK

NONSENSE!

YOU HAVE TO EAT, ARI.

clank

ARE YOU OKAY?

I WAS WORRIED ABOUT YOU, YOU KNOW.

I KNOW. I'M SORRY.

SSSSSHHH

DAD. WHAT ARE YOU DOING?

I'M MAKING FOOD!

WELL, COME OVER HERE. I NEED TO TALK TO YOU GUYS.

OKAY.

DO YOU REMEMBER WHEN THE BAKERY BURNED DOWN?

YES, ARI. WE REMEMBER WHEN THE BAKERY BURNED DOWN.

NO. YEAH. OF COURSE YOU DO.

THAT'S NOT WHAT I MEANT.

I GUESS I MEAN... DO YOU REMEMBER WHEN I SAID IT WAS HECTOR'S FAULT?

WELL, IT WASN'T.

IT WAS OUR FAULT.

IT WAS *MY* FAULT.

311

OH, ARI.

AND I HURT HIM. AND I MISS HIM.

AND I HURT YOU GUYS.

I JUST MESSED EVERYTHING UP.

SNIFF

OH, BABY.

IT'S OKAY.

SOB

I DON'T KNOW IF YOU REMEMBER, BUT WHEN YOU WERE A LITTLE KID, YOU USED TO LOVE TO BAKE WITH ME.

...BUT I FEEL LIKE YOU LOST THAT SOMEWHERE ALONG THE WAY.

TSSSS

AND I FELT LIKE I LOST YOU.

LOST MY BOY.

BUT THEN SOMETHING HAPPENED THIS SUMMER.

YOU WERE LIKE YOUR OLD SELF FOR A LITTLE WHILE.

AND I TRIED TO FIGURE OUT WHAT WAS DIFFERENT, AND I REALIZED...

...IT WAS THE BOY. HECTOR.

SHAKE

HE HELPED YOU FIND THAT HAPPINESS YOU USED TO HAVE.

SHAKE

SO, I DON'T KNOW WHAT IT MEANS.

MAYBE JUST...DON'T TRY TO BE WHAT YOU THINK YOU SHOULD BE.

BE WHAT YOU LOVE.

OKAY.
IT'S LATE. I'M
GOING TO SLEEP.

PHAHA

OH MY
GOD.

OKAY.

LOVE YOU,
DAD.

munch
munch

IT'S GOOD TO
HAVE YOU BACK
HOME, ARI.

LOVE YOU.

NOW GET
SOME SLEEP.

IT'S
ALMOST
3 AM.

HEY, YOU!

WHAT ARE YOU GUYS DOING HERE?

YOUR MOM TEXTED US IN THE MIDDLE OF THE NIGHT AND TOLD US YOU WERE BACK.

REALLY?

I DIDN'T EVEN KNOW MY MOM KNEW HOW TO TEXT.

I WAS GOING TO TELL YOU GUYS I WAS BACK, BY THE WAY.

I WAS ACTUALLY WORRIED YOU WOULDN'T STILL BE HERE.

SPLOOSH

WHERE ARE WE GONNA GO?

I DON'T KNOW.

SCHOOL? BACKPACKING ACROSS EUROPE?

EVERYTHING SEEMS LIKE IT'S CHANGING SO FAST.

OH, WELL, WE *ARE* BOTH GOING TO SCHOOL.

WAIT, WHAT?

YEAH!

BUT WE'RE NOT MOVING AWAY OR ANYTHING.

WE'RE STICKING AROUND HERE FOR SCHOOL, BUD!

OH JEEZ.

GOOD!

I DON'T WANT YOU GUYS TO MOVE AWAY.

IS THAT SELFISH?

NO WAY!

I LIKE HAVING YOU GUYS AROUND, TOO.

IT'S TRUE. WE'RE THE BEST.

JUST GRAB ANYTHING YOU WANT TO KEEP AND WE'LL LOAD IT INTO THE VAN.

WE NEED TO GET EVERYTHING WE'RE KEEPING OUT BEFORE THEY START REBUILDING!

NO.

I'M JUST GONNA GRAB THE MOPED.

I'LL MEET YOU GUYS BACK AT THE MOTEL?

SOUNDS GOOD TO ME.

Ha Ha

NO NEED TO LOCK IT UP, I GUESS.

HI.

I'M SORRY.

YOU LET ME GO, ARI.

YOU USED ME TO GET WHAT YOU WANTED, WHATEVER THAT WAS, AND THEN...

...AND THEN YOU JUST FORGOT ABOUT ME.

I DIDN'T FORGET ABOUT YOU.

NOT FOR ONE SECOND.

THEN WHAT HAPPENED?

YOU NEVER EVEN TRIED TO CALL ME.

I DIDN'T THINK YOU WOULD WANT TO TALK TO ME.

BUT YOU DIDN'T EVEN *TRY!*

I'M—

AND THE WORST PART IS, I WOULD HAVE FORGIVEN YOU.

BUT WHY?

I MESSED UP SO BAD.

WHY WOULD YOU EVER FORGIVE ME?

BECAUSE I LIKE BEING AROUND YOU, ARI.

YOU'RE FUNNY, YOU'RE EARNEST, YOU'RE DETERMINED.

AND DESPITE ALL THE STUPID STUFF YOU DO, I CAN'T HELP BUT ROOT FOR YOU.

SNIFF

I'M SORRY.

I PROMISE.

I'M SO SORRY, HECTOR.

HEY!

IT'S SO COLD!

LOOK WHO WE FOUND!

OHHH. I MISSED YOU!

Ha Ha

I MISSED YOU, TOO!

I'M SO EXCITED TO BE HERE.

SCHOOL IS GREAT, BUT I'M READY FOR THIS VACATION!

MEG SAYS HI, BY THE WAY.

WOW!

LOOK AT THIS PLACE!

OH, YEAH! YOU HAVEN'T SEEN IT YET!

HOW HAVE YOU NOT SEEN THIS BEAUTIFUL NEW BAKERY, HECTOR?

ARI HAS BEEN WORKING SO HARD ON IT!

I'VE BEEN AT SCHOOL, HANNA.

TA-DA!

YEAH.

WE HAVE GOOD INSURANCE.

HAH

IT'S ALL SO FANCY.

AND THIS THING WORKS NOW?

YEP.

IT WAS THE FIRST THING WE FIXED.

DAD CHECKED IT LIKE THIRTY-EIGHT TIMES.

OKAY. WE'RE GOING UPSTAIRS NOW.

YOU GUYS HAVE FUN.

Peek

heh

I CAN'T BELIEVE YOU'RE *HERE*.

ONLY FOR A WEEK, THOUGH.

DON'T REMIND ME.

I'M GLAD YOU DECIDED TO GO BACK TO SCHOOL.

IF IT MAKES YOU HAPPY, IT MAKES ME HAPPY.

AND I'M REALLY PROUD OF ALL THE WORK I'VE BEEN DOING ON THE BAKERY.

AWWWW. YOU DORK.

I'M PROUD OF YOU, TOO.

OKAY!

I WANNA GO SEE EVERYBODY!

GUESS WHO'S HERE!

HECTOR!

HEY! IT'S EVERYBODY!

MR. KYRKOS! I'VE GOT SOMETHING FOR YOU.

?

FOR ME?

I THOUGHT THIS MIGHT HELP OUT WHEN YOU REOPEN.

KYRKOS FAMILY ♥ SOURDOUGH STARTER

OH MY!

BUT HOW—?

YOU ARE A TRUE ANGEL!

SMAK SMAK

HELEN!

LOOK!

HA HA

Thanks for reading *Bloom*!

Baking and music are such a big part of this book. While working on *Bloom*, we would make the food baked by the characters and send each other music in order to help find the right tone for every scene. So when First Second asked us about what extras we wanted to put in the back of the book, it made perfect sense to include a recipe and a playlist, along with some production art!

Thanks again for reading, and we hope you enjoy baking the Kyrkos Family Bakery's Famous Sourdough Rolls as much as Ari and Hector did! Why not put on some tunes while you cook?

Savanna & Kevin

Special thanks to Nick, Brook, Stephen, Charlie, James, Paulina, and all our friends and family who made *Bloom* possible!

KYRKOS FAMILY BAKERY'S
Famous Sourdough Rolls

Ingredients:

1 cup sourdough starter (fresh)

1 cup whole wheat flour

2 ¼ teaspoons (one package) active dry yeast

2 teaspoons salt

3 tablespoons brown sugar

1 cup warm (110°F / 43°C) water

¼ cup melted butter

2 cups bread flour

1 tablespoon olive oil

1 egg

1 tablespoon water

Steps:

1. In a large bowl, mix starter, whole wheat flour, yeast, salt, and brown sugar until combined.
2. Stir in warm water and melted butter.
3. Stir in bread flour ½ cup at a time until a dough is formed.
4. Knead dough on a floured surface for 10 minutes until it becomes shiny and springy to the touch.
5. Oil the sides of a large bowl with the olive oil. Place the dough in the large oiled bowl and cover. Keep in a warm spot until the dough doubles in size (approximately 2 hours).
6. On a floured surface, punch dough down lightly to flatten. Cut dough into 10 equal-sized pieces and roll into balls.
7. Cut a simple leaf design (just barely) into the tops of the rolls.
8. Place dough balls on parchment-lined pan at least 2 inches apart.
9. Keep in a warm spot until the dough doubles in size again (approximately 1 hour).
10. Preheat oven to 400°F / 204°C.
11. Brush the top of the buns with egg wash (a mixture of 1 beaten egg and 1 tablespoon of water).
12. Bake rolls in oven for 25 minutes.
13. Remove the rolls and check the bottoms. They should be a rich brown color and sound hollow when you tap on them. If they're not ready, just pop the rolls back in and check them again at 3-minute intervals until they're done.

Production Art

Bloom pitch pages

I LOVE GRAPHIC NOVELS!

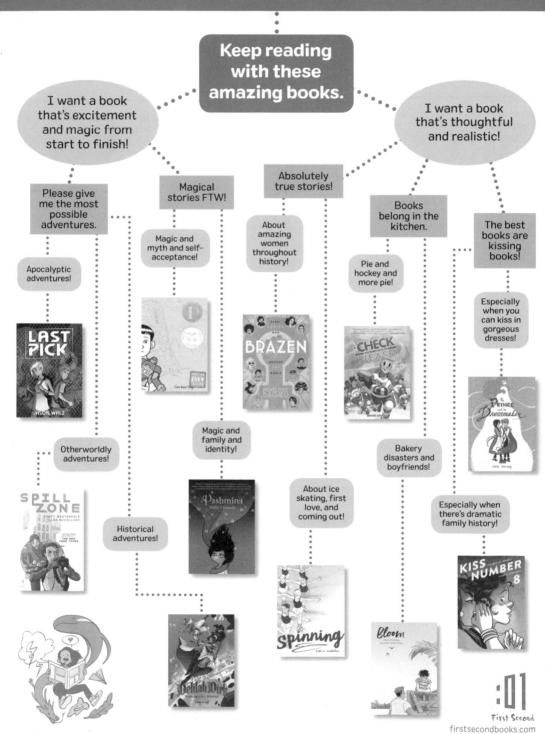

Keep reading with these amazing books.

I want a book that's excitement and magic from start to finish!

I want a book that's thoughtful and realistic!

Please give me the most possible adventures.

Magical stories FTW!

Absolutely true stories!

Books belong in the kitchen.

The best books are kissing books!

Apocalyptic adventures!

Magic and myth and self-acceptance!

About amazing women throughout history!

Pie and hockey and more pie!

Especially when you can kiss in gorgeous dresses!

LAST PICK
JASON WALZ

BRAZEN
PENELOPE BAGIEU

CHECK PLEASE!

The PRINCE and the Dressmaker
Jen Wang

Otherworldly adventures!

Magic and family and identity!

Bakery disasters and boyfriends!

SPILL ZONE
SCOTT WESTERFELD
ALEX PUVILLAND
THE NEW YORK TIMES

Pashmina
Nidhi Chanani

About ice skating, first love, and coming out!

Especially when there's dramatic family history!

Historical adventures!

spinning
tillie walden

Bloom

KISS NUMBER 8

Delilah Dirk

:01
First Second
firstsecondbooks.com